Miracles in Progress

Miracles in Progress

A Compilation of Christian Writings

Raymond Mears

To order additional copies of this book, contact:
Xlibris Corporation
1-888-795-4274
www.Xlibris.com
Orders@Xlibris.com
76711

Contents

Dedication

It is with humility and loving gratitude that I dedicate this work to my family, friends and loved ones who have given me encouragement and with kind words have urged me to bring this book to fruition. I am sure, though, they will all understand when I say the One who is truly responsible for the existence of this book is my Father in Heaven, the Almighty God, to whom all the glory and honor is due. Amen.

Raymond Mears

Foreword

It is impossible to write about what you don't know. Sure, one can use one's imagination, but there must be a basic foundation of knowledge or fact from which to draw. As readers go through this collection of stories, it is my prayer that they will be enriched with the knowledge that they are not alone in the problems they face or the lives they live. As we go through life, we all need to be aware of a greater power at work in our lives. Not one of these stories would ever have been written without inspiration from God. And so the Christian Stories are an attempt to show the reader what Christ has meant in my life. Whether we admit it or not, we are all a part of the family of God, created by Him in His image. It is our loss if we reject Him and His Son, Jesus.

Christian Short Stories

The Journey

Chapter One

Willie was cold, bitterly cold. He had never been so cold! The snow was falling much heavier now and he was walking by instinct. Surely the town couldn't be much farther. As cold as he was, Willie felt a warmth deep inside as he looked at the small girl now wrapped in his fur coat and sleeping soundly in his arms. The eerie silence of the falling snow just made him that much more aware of the situation. If only the wind would die down a little he knew he would be able to find the town, because the whiteness of the snow would give plenty of light to see by. By now he knew it was late and would be dark. He was very tired and he had to fight to keep from stopping to rest. The temperature was dropping now and he must not stop. He had heard too many stories of people who died when they stopped moving in a snow storm. But the load he was carrying now was precious and helpless and he knew her only chance to live rested in him. Willie was a young man, strong and full of life. At the age of twenty-four he knew it was time he began to seriously consider marrying. There was, after all, Kathy, and he had been running from her long enough. He knew he loved her and that she loved him. It was just that she was forever talking about Jesus. Just like his mother! Now Willie had a heart big as all outdoors and he could accept "love thy neighbor", but a virgin birth and raised from the dead? Didn't make any sense to him. As he struggled through the snow he thought back to the events of the night and the fix he was in. The circumstance of how he had found the little girl was a miracle and now he needed another miracle if he was to save her and himself. Had there really been a man? If so, where had he disappeared to? He had been driving home, trying to beat the storm that was now raging all around him, when the man had suddenly appeared in front of him on the road. He had barely seen him in time to swerve to miss him. The swerve became a slide and into the roadside ditch he went! Attempting to back out of the ditch he realized he would never make it without help. Getting out of the car he had walked back up to the road to see if the man were all right, only there was no man! Looking all around he could see nothing except the road, the car, and the snow as it began to fall heavier. He started back to the car but something caught his eye and as he looked he could see a faint light in the field across the road. He called out but heard no answer and was going to call out again when he realized he could neither hear or be heard in this wind. He started walking toward the faint light and suddenly it was gone! "Hello, is anyone there?" he called. Getting no answer, he was beginning to think it was all a dream and he would waken any minute now. As he turned to walk back to the car, his foot caught on something and he almost fell. He looked down to see a dark bundle almost entirely covered by the falling snow. Bending down to see what it was, he heard a low moan. He quickly brushed away the snow and that's when he had found the little girl. Completely forgetting everything else, he brushed the snow from her and covered her with his coat. He could tell she was alive and he was sure she was sleeping and not unconscious. And now here he was somewhere between his car and the town. Plodding through the ever deepening snow he wondered who the little girl was and how she had come to be all alone in such place and in such a storm. Thinking of her helplessness, he thought back to his own childhood. Being a poor, black, skinny child, he had faced many unpleasant situations, but nothing like the plight of this little girl. He had never known his father, but his God-fearing momma had been a rock in his life. She taught him responsibility, respect for others and hard work. Only thing was, she kept talking about Jesus and how much He loved me remembered Willie. But I always wondered where He was when I was having to work and get food for my momma and brothers and sisters. "Fact is, I wonder where He is now." Willie said into the howling wind. "Cause He can see this fix I'm in and, if it was only me, I figure I could probably make on my own, but I can't take no chance with this little girl and me 'n her shore need some help." After he had been walking for what seemed hours he finally realized he just had to stop and rest. He found a place just below a small knoll and began to scoop out a place in the snow where the hill had kept it from piling up too high. What made him do it he never knew, but he took off his red bandana and tying it to a small limb he stuck it in the snow atop the knoll. Then lying down and holding the little girl as close as he could he thought "I'll just rest a few minutes and then we'll go on. Now Lord don't let me sleep too long and fail this little one.

Chapter Two

Jack and Helen Martin were two very happy people. They were happily married and were very much in love even after eight years. Little Lisa was asleep in the back seat and she was the apple of their eyes. As they drove along the country road on their way to Larksville, Jack turned to Helen and said, "We don't have far to go and well be there long before the "norther" hits. The way those clouds look, it'll probably snow." "Oh, look" said Helen, "at the pretty wild flowers in the field there. It's such a shame to be so pretty and then be killed by an old snow storm. Let's stop and pick some. Then we'll have them a little longer to remember the autumn and the colors". "All right," said Jack. Looking to see that Lisa was still fast asleep, they quietly left the car and went to pick the flowers. After a few minutes, Jack looked up at the now threatening sky and said, "We'd better go. It's gonna snow. I can feel it in the wind." Laughing like two teenagers, they ran back to the car and soon were once more on the way toLarksville. Lisa Martin came awake at the sound of the car door closing. Looking out the window she saw Mommy and Daddy walking to the field on the other side of the road. As she watched them picking flowers, she said "I want a bouquet too." Getting out of the car, she saw some flowers on her side of the road and ran to get her own bouquet. As she picked the little yellow flowers she thought Mommy would be very proud of her. Suddenly she heard the car start and looking up she saw the car drive off down the road! Running as fast as she could, fighting back the tears, she cried "Daddy, Mommy, wait for me." But it was too late. When she reached the road the car was almost out of sight. Little five year old Lisa was all alone. Crying, she sat down with the flowers still clutched in her little hand. Then she thought, surely they'll see I'm gone and they'll come back for me. Feeling reassured, she began to sing the little song she had learned in Sunday School, "Jesus loves me, this I know, for the bible tells me so." After what seemed a long time they still had not returned. Feeling the first few flakes of snow, she walked back to the edge of the field and lay in the taller grass to try to keep warm. Remembering the song, she said, "Jesus I know you love me, so please help me. Let them come back for me." Then crying softly, she fell asleep.

As they drove into the driveway of his parents home in Larksville, Jack saw them standing on the front porch, eagerly awaiting their arrival. Getting out of the car, Jack and Helen ran to greet them with hugs and kisses. "Better come on in out of this wind" his dad said., "I think it's gonna snow." After a few minutes his mother said, "Where's Lisa?" "Oh my" said Jack, "She's still asleep in the car. I'll go get her." He returned quickly saying "She's not there. Did she come in?" "No we haven't seen her" said his mother. "She probably woke up and is out back with the dog" said Jack's father, "You know how she loves old Tippy". Walking to the back door he called "Lisa, Lisa, come in darling, it's starting to snow." There no answer. Now beginning to get worried, they all left the house and began to look for her. The snow began to fall in earnest now. When they had searched everywhere without finding her, Helen was in a state of near hysteria. "We'll find her" Jack said, "she can't have gone far. We have to remain calm. Dad you call the neighbors and ask them to help form a search party." An hour later, looking for the tenth time in the car, Jack saw the forgotten flowers on the car seat. "Oh no," he said "surely not." He told his parents of the stop by the roadside to pick the flowers and said, "Truthfully, I don't remember seeing her since then." His dad called the sheriff and within a few minutes a caravan of cars started back down the road out of Larksville. They had gotten less than half a mile when it became clear the road was impassible. As they turned the car around something caught in the headlights and Jack said "What's that?" "What?" said his dad, "Over there, in the field" said Jack, "It's something red." Trudging through the snow they came upon a stick with a red bandana tied to it. As he wondered what it was there for, Jack noticed a large mound of snow just below the knoll. As realization set in, he scrambled down the hill and began to dig. Within a few seconds he had found Lisa. And she was wrapped in a big, furry coat, lying in the arms of a strange man. Willie awoke with a start! He tried to raise himself up, saying "I got to keep goin, I got to keep goin." Suddenly he felt strong hands pushing him firmly but gently back down and he realized he was on a bed. Opening his eyes, he saw a stranger staring down at him, smiling broadly. "Hello" the man said, "I'm Doctor Thomas. I see our hero has finally decided to rejoin the living. Now, maybe we can find out just who you are!" "Where am I" asked Willie, "Where am I and where's the little girl?" "She's just fine" said the Doctor, "and you are in the hospital. You saved her life you know, She and her parents were on a trip to town and they decided to stop and pick some wild flowers knowing the coming storm would soon kill them. She was sleeping in the back seat." Then he told Willie the whole story of how she had been accidentally left. "You must have found her shortly after that. But I must say, I'd like to know just how in the world you found her in that storm. We almost didn't find you but that red bandana showed up in our lights. You had carried her almost ten miles and were just five hundred yards from the edge of the town. You are quite a hero, you know."

Chapter Three

Willie Clower sits beneath the huge oak tree on the city square, watching the crowd of Christmas shoppers go by. Wiping a tear from his eye, he remembers the episode of the little girl, Lisa Martin. As the dead leaves all around him rustle in the freshening wind, he recalls that it was really cold that night. He reaches down and tugs at the leather coverings on the stubs of what were his legs and sighs. "Reckon nobody ever thinks 'bout that night no more 'cept me, "he said. "I shore didn't know my legs wuz freezin that night," he thinks, "but it wouldn't a made no difference. I had to save that little girl. And besides, Lord," he says, looking upward to the sky, "something more than that little girl got saved that night. Reckon getting my soul saved was worth two legs anyway. When me and that little girl hunkered down below that little hill, You remember how I really prayed for the first time in my life. I tried to remember how my momma prayed, and all the things she taught me about You started coming back to me. And me and Kathy had a good life serving you Lord, til you took her on home. Ain't no way I'm ever gonna complain with all the blessings I've had in my life! And you still bless me Father. Why I done already sold enough pencils today to buy me food for a month. I know I'm gittin old and gray, but Lord I'll be ready when you call me home. And Lord, my legs, I really didn't mind losin them for the sake of that little girl. Besides, it made it real easy to stay humble and on my knees before you. And Father, thank you for sending that angel that night to lead me to the girl." Willie rearranges the pencils layed out before him and leans back against the little wall. The passersby would take a pencil and put the money in his cup as he lay sleeping. They would wonder at the smile on his face. What they didn't know was that at that very moment in a Heaven far away, Willie was hearing his Father God say, "Well done my son, welcome home"

The Still, Small Voice

It was very early in the morning, just before first light. He had awakened with a start as though something was wrong. Though it was his custom to rise very early, he felt different and he didn't know why. Pouring some water into the clay bowl by his bed, he rinsed his face and hands and began to dress himself. As he slipped his feet into his sandals, he thought of the boat and wondered if today would be better than the day before. It had been a long time since they'd had a real good catch. Fishing for a living was never easy. The work was hard at best and when the catch was small, it seemed the hard work was for nothing. Making his way down the path to the sea and the boat, he considered the life he lived. He was a big man, strong and able and he enjoyed the physical aspect of fishing. The lowering of the nets, pulling them in loaded with fish, and the good companions he had working with him, but sometimes it seemed a still, small voice would speak inside him saying "This is not your destiny." As he had done so often in the past when he thought of the voice, he wondered what it was. Since he was just a boy the voice had been with him. Sometimes it was just a sudden feeling to make a different decision or take a different way. Sometimes it came in the night as a dream or vision, telling him what he needed to do or where life might lead him. He had never understood what it was or where it came from, but the conviction in him was always so strong, he always obeyed. He reached the boat just as dawn was breaking and saw that some of the others were there before him. There was a mist rising softly over the sea as his brother Andy came walking toward him. "Today is gonna be great." Andy said. "I think we'll have a big catch." "Well," he answered, "it sure needs to be. I don't know how much longer I want to do this if it doesn't get better." They had put out from the shore and were just lowering their nets when they saw a man walking by the shore. The stranger stopped and looked at them. His first thought was to ignore the stranger but the small voice was there once again, saying "Listen to him." The stranger lifted his hand toward them and said "Come and follow me." Again his first thought was to ignore him but the small voice said "Go." Against all reason and logic, he and his brother immediately left the boat and followed him. Once more, he obeyed the still, small voice inside him and he became one of the best known men in the history of the world. His name was Peter, his brother was Andrew, and the stranger was JESUS. Because of his obedience to the still, small voice, Simon Peter was not only the man God meant him to be but he was in the right place at the right time. Always listen to the small voice that's in you and obey for; "In all your ways acknowledge Him and He shall direct your paths." (Proverbs 3:3)

The Beginning

Lester W. Stonebridge III, what a beginning! Surely his parents expected great things of him to have given him such a name. Why someday he would be a great man and great men must have great names. But then his parents were probably no different than most parents when their first born is a bouncing baby boy. He was glad they couldn't see him now, for "Stoney" Stonebridge would never be mistaken for greatness. As he shifted his position on the pile of brown wrapping paper next to the dumpster, he began to recall his life and what had happened that would cause him to come to this.

Was it really 28 years ago it all began? How could so much go so wrong in so short a time? It had started off well enough. His father had a good income, they lived in a nice neighborhood and his mother doted on him. Love was never something he missed. He knew his parents loved him and even his sister, two years his junior, loved him so much he was her idol. Oh yes, and Grandma. She was his haven in times of stress. She used to sit him on her lap and tell him bible stories and how much Jesus loved him. Boy, was that some fairy tale! And to think, at the time he really believed her. Scratching his scraggly beard, he fumbled in the paper and found the bottle. Man, just enough for one more drink! Putting the bottle to his lips, he finished it. Arranging the paper as best he could into a pillow of sorts, he closed his eyes and slept. His last thought as he went to sleep was "I sure wish Grandma had been right. I could use a little love about now."

"Stoney, Stoney" He came awake hearing someone call his name. Sitting up he looked to see who was calling him. Seeing no one and thinking it was just another time the booze had him hearing things, he started to lay down to resume his sleep when he became aware of his surroundings. He couldn't see the dumpster and there were no papers around him! Getting to his feet he looked around. Where was he? As far as the eye could see there was nothing! Just an eerie whiteness all around him. "Wow", he said, "I shouldn't have taken that last drink. I'm really tripping out now."

Suddenly he heard that voice again. "Stoney, Stoney". Looking around he saw someone coming toward him. He couldn't recognize who it was but they were surely calling his name. As the figures drew nearer, he could see there were two of them. All at once recognition set in. It was Pete and Hal who had served with him in Desert Storm. It hadn't been much of a war as wars go but it had been all too real to him. Hugging them close he thought how good it was to see them again. He hadn't seen them since that tank battle. He remembered seeing their tank take a direct hit.

"Wait a minute!" "Hey what are you guys doin here? You're dead!" "Sure we are" Hal said "and so are you". "I'm dead? No way, I'm just passed out." "No, you're really dead" said Pete, "well almost anyway. You see they have to check the records and all to make sure there's no mistake, but they almost never make a mistake so you're dead. It's really not so bad here once you get used to it. It's really neat to watch the new ones coming in. Never know when you'll see someone you knew. Why just last week we saw your Mom and Dad and your sister." "What do you mean?," asked Stoney, "my family is OK. I'm the bad one." "Yes," said Pete, "but we've learned a lot up here. It seems when you live a bad life it always affects others and usually those closest to you. You see when you let the bad memories of the war and your buddies getting killed lead you to become an addict and an alcoholic, you thought you were only hurting yourself. But the truth is your sister thought that if you took drugs it must be OK and she over-dosed. On the way to the hospital, your Mom and Dad were killed in an accident. And all because of you and the life you lived."

Stoney came awake sobbing violently. There was the dumpster. It had all been a dream. Thank God, maybe there was still time to change. Wait a minute. What did I say? Thank God? Grabbing hold of the dumpster, he pulled himself to a kneeling position and with tears streaming down his face he said, "Dear god, if you're real, if Grandma really did know you, and if there really was a Jesus, help me!" Then from somewhere deep within his spirit Stoney, for the first time, heard the voice of God. "Stop crying my son and be not afraid for I have already heard your prayer. My Word says "Knock and it shall be opened to you, ask and ye shall receive. I heard your knock. I heard you ask." "When did I knock and when did I ask?" asked Stoney? And the Lord said "When you were going to sleep and remembering your Grandmother, you said you could use a little love. It's just that simple. Just ask. Now I have seen fit to give you a glimpse of what the future could be. It's up to you to make sure it doesn't happen that way," "What can I do" asked Stoney, And the Lord said "In my Word, I said it this way. Take up" your cross and follow me, To you I say, Repent, go home, Your family will welcome you with open arms. Repent means to change your life completely and never again sin,"

Pastor Lester W. Stonebridge III looks out over his congregation, smiling as he remembers from where the Lord delivered him, I may not be a great man he thinks, but I'm great in the kingdom of God.

The beginning,

The Letter

Chapter One

THE SON

As he sat there reading the letter, tears streamed down his cheeks and dropped to the pages, adding to the tear stains already there from long ago. It was obvious the worn pages had been read and cried over many times over the years. The story they told was very special and one he had never heard. He had found the letter in the big old trunk in the attic where he now sat. "Oh Mom," he thought, "why did you never share this with me?" They had buried his Mother three days ago and now, after the shock and grief had begun to wear off, he had started the slow and arduous task of going through the house, finding and cataloging items that he would dispose of, or keep, or maybe send to his sister. He had known the job would be a sad one but he hadn't counted on something like this letter! The newspaper clipping folded neatly in the envelope with the letter told a story that was both heartwarming and sad, but the letter really was the answer to questions he had wondered about all his life.

THE MOTHER

Betty Marlin was just about as happy as a body could be! Her life with Hal was everything she had hoped it would be, except for the times he had to be away at sales conventions. Sitting in the bedroom in the little house they had just bought, she marveled at the way her life was going. She was expecting their first child and now they had a real home, with a bedroom she could fix up for the baby. As she sat on the floor next to the big trunk that had been her hope chest, she carefully placed the things in their proper place. "I'm going to keep everything about our life together and someday our children will have a record of all the wonderful things that have happened and will happen in our lives," she thought to herself. "Oh look, here's our marriage license, Harold Marlin and Elisabeth Coulter were joined together in Holy Matrimony on . . . Oh I must get a frame for this." As she moved to get more items to store in the trunk, she felt the movement inside her and said aloud, "Now you just don't get in too big a hurry little Roger Marlin. Oh I just know it will be a boy."

THE FATHER

In Reno, Nevada, Hal Marlin had just checked out of the hotel and was on his way to the railway station. "I'm sure glad the convention is over. Now I can be home with Betty when the baby comes," he thought. He reached into his coat pocket to make sure the letter wasn't still there. Yep, he had mailed it. Wouldn't have been the first time he had forgotten to mail a letter, and Betty didn't like that. He would be on the train for two days before he reached

Gatlinburg and then another half a day in a buggy to get to the little farm. It was coming on to December and would be getting real cold anytime now. "I sure will have to get busy to make sure the house is fixed up to be nice and warm for the baby," Looking up he said "Lord I hope it's a boy but just let it be a healthy baby and I won't complain."

Boarding the train, he found his way to his seat and began to prepare for the long trip home.

THE CIRCUMSTANCE

In Glenwood canyon, some two hundred miles west of Denver, the eerie quiet of heavily falling snow was shattered by the awful sound of an avalanche. Thundering down the side of the mountain, carrying trees and boulders, it hit the railway bridge full force. When once again all was quiet, the bridge was gone!

Chapter Two

In the line shack, the young cowboy woke with a start! "What on earth was that," he wondered. A very loud noise had wakened him. "Must a been a slide in the canyon," he thought, "I'd better go check the fence. Don't want no cows getting down by the tracks and getting hit by a train." Old Rabbit, his horse, wasn't too keen on the idea of a cold bit being stuck into his mouth and the feel of the blanket and saddle just meant the warm barn and sleeping were things of the past. He had to admit though, that Wes Stone, his owner, took mighty good care of him, and didn't like getting out this time of night any more'n he did so it must be important. Okay, he wouldn't act up this time! Making their way cautiously down the side of the mountain, they reached the bottom and Wes started to check the fence. After about a quarter of a mile, he found where the avalanche had gone through the fence. "Wow, I'd a liked to been here to seen that one," He thought. Following the path of the slide with his eyes he saw what was left of the railway bridge. Nothing! "Rabbit," he said to the horse, "I know you ain't a gonna like this and I don't much cotton to the idea myself, but we got to get on down to the telegraph and let them know what's happened."

Wes knew every foot of this country and he knew it would be difficult getting to the telegraph station three miles down the track, but if his sense of time was right it was about one-thirty in the morning and the three o'clock from the west would have to be flagged down. It had begun to snow again and large, heavy, wet flakes found their way to his face as he rode into the wind. After roughly a half a mile of plodding through the snow, it had gotten so bad he couldn't see the tracks and they were within three feet of where Rabbit was walking! Wes knew it would do no good for he and Rabbit to get lost or slip and get hurt. There would be no way for anyone to even know they were out in this storm, much less find them. Knowing the urgency of the situation he didn't want to stop but if he didn't, he and Rabbit would be in serious danger. Gingerly, he led his horse closer to the cliffs that rose above the tracks, looking for someplace they could get out of the wind. He got out of the saddle and kept walking, leading Rabbit with one hand and holding the other hand out toward the face of the cliff. Then, as if by magic, he couldn't touch the rocks of the cliff and he knew that meant there was a cut-back in the rock. Maybe it would be big enough for him and the horse to squeeze into and get out of the wind. Easing into the cut-back, he found that it was more than big enough and at the back there was even a little overhang of the rock that formed sort of a shallow cave! "We're shore in luck Rabbit," he said to the horse as he led him into the little cave. "Let me see if I can find a little drift wood in the snow and I'll get us a fire goin." Half and hour later, as he hunkered by the fire, he thought of the railway bridge. "If this wind will just let up a little, maybe we can still get to the telegraph on time," he thought, "but I know I'd never find it in this storm." A couple of miles down the track, 'Turkey leg" Jackson, the telegrapher, slept in his chair by the warm fire, completely unaware of the magnitude of the storm raging just outside the door.

Gilmore Smoley, engineer of the Western Limited out of San Francisco, stared glumly out of the window of the engine into the falling snow. A little while earlier, they had passed through Grand :Junction and were now about to enter Glenwood Canyon where the tracks followed the Colorado River as it wound it's way through the canyon. On the other side of the river, he knew, was the highway, but now he could see no lights through the snow. "Anybody'd be a fool to be on the road in this storm," : he thought, "it's bad enough here in the cab of this engine." But Gil had made this run many times in 'his years as an engineer and he knew they would be able to make Glenwood Springs before the snow got too bad. Still, he knew he must remain alert, because you never knew what could happen in a snow storm like this. As this thought crossed his mind, he realized that two sets of eyes were better than one, so he woke up young Jimmy, his fireman. "I know you were all comfy and cozy, but I think you'd best help me keep an eye out on the tracks up ahead. It's snowing pretty good!" he said, once Jimmy was awake enough to understand him. "Maybe you'd better get on the wire and see how things are up ahead." In the shack ahead, 'Turkey leg' kept right on sleeping, never hearing the chattering telegraph key! No one east of the little telegraph shack heard either as the wire was down near where the bridge had been. "I'm not getting any response" Jimmy said. "Must be the line is down somewhere," said Gil, "but we can't stop in this storm. Just help me keep a sharp watch. We'll be in Glenwood Springs in a little while and we'll find out there how bad the storm is. If we have to, we'll stay there til it blows over."

In a few miles, Gil could see a light up ahead. The falling snow had ceased for the moment and he could just make out the telegrapher's shack as they passed. "Old 'Turkey leg' is sleeping again," he said to Jimmy. "Can't say as I blame him. The snow has let up, so I'm gonna get up a little more speed while we can see." As they rounded a bend a few miles up the track, Jimmy heard Gil scream. "Oh my God," cried Gil, "the bridge is out!" Frantically, he used all the knowledge he possessed and did every thing he could to stop the train, but it was too late. Gil's last thought as the engine flew into the space where the bridge had been was "God help us!"

Chapter Three

The young cowboy, Wes Stone and his horse, Rabbit had left the shallow cave just as soon as the snow let up and were within a hundred yards of the telegraph shack when the 3 o'clock from the west roared by. "Oh my Lord," Wes said to Rabbit, "We got real trouble now." He started to turn back to where he knew the train would wreck, but he suddenly realized his help alone would do little and with the telegraph they could send for help from the railroad. Then he could go to the home ranch which was about 3 miles away and get the other hands to get some wagons and load them with medicine and blankets and supplies. Getting down from his horse, he pushed into the shack and woke up 'Turkey leg' to get him on the telegraph. As he was explaining, they heard the awful sound of the crash that was three miles away! Leaving 'Turkey leg' to work with the telegraph key, Wes mounted Rabbit and headed to the ranch. In spite of the urgency of the situation, Wes had to smile remembering 'Turkey leg' hopping around the little shack. He could sure see where he got his name. He looked for all the world like a turkey with one leg tied to a post as he moved about, flopping his elbows!

In his Pullman berth, Hal Marlin woke with a sense of foreboding. "What is it Lord?" he asked. "Do I need to pray?" Getting out of the berth, he slipped on his shoes and walked to the back of the car. He got into the little vestibule between the cars and looked out the window. He could see it had been snowing and that there seemed to be a cliff next to the tracks. Again, he asked "Lord, what do you want me to do? I feel in my spirit it was You who woke me up." About that time he lurched against the wall as the brakes of the train locked up and he heard the screeching of the wheels on the rails. Realizing the train was in trouble, he went to the river side of the car and saw there was a gently falling away slope on that side. Quickly, he opened the door and jumped just as the awful sound of the engine crashing came to his ears.

Rolling over and over in the snow, he came to a stop and watched as the cars roared by one by one and followed the engine into the abyss. Jumping up, he ran down the tracks toward the train, noticing the last car had not gone over the edge. There was already the sound of cries for help from the wreckage of the train, along with moans and the hiss of escaping steam. There seemed to be no fire. As the people from the last car started to get off the train, he noticed that most were still in their sleeping clothes as he was and he knew they would become aware of the intense cold any minute now. Knowing the first priority would be to get those who were unhurt to help those who were injured, he stopped the mass exodus from the car, Yelling to be heard above the storm, he told them to get back in the car and get their warmest clothes on because they were needed to help in the rescue. At first there were cries of fear that the car would go over the edge, but he reassured them in a firm voice that there was no danger and to do as they were told! Walking up to a large, heavy-set man who had evidently been clothed and awake at the time of the accident, he asked him his name. "Jack Hedge" he said. "Well Jack," said Hal, "You and I have our work cut out for us. We have to get the ones who are uninjured organized and help those others down there. Thanks to the snow we can see pretty well."

Deep down at the bottom of the draw, engineer Gil Smoley lay bleeding and in great pain. He didn't know how bad he was hurt, but his one thought was try to move and find young Jimmy. Moving with great difficulty, he got to his feet and found he could stand without any pain in his legs. His left arm felt funny and he supposed it was broken. He opened his jacket a bit and put his left hand inside to immobilize his arm as best he could, then started toward the engine which was a few feet away from where he had been thrown. The steam had all escaped into the air, the fire was out and now, in the eerie whiteness and silence of the lightly falling snow, the moans and cries of the injured and dying could be heard. At the engine he could see no sign of Jimmy. Turning to go back to the first wrecked car, he stumbled and looked down into the unseeing eyes of Jimmy as the softly falling snow began to cover him. Knowing he was dead and that he couldn't help him, he made himself move on toward the sound of the injured. The car, first behind the coal tender, had come to rest on it's side, with one end up on the coal car and the other end down on the rocks. As he approached he saw a young boy pulling on the arm of someone inside the car. He climbed up to where the young lad was pulling and sobbing. Hearing him, the boy turned and cried "Help me, it's Momma".

Gil looked down into the car and saw a young woman who was seemingly pinned in the wreckage of the seat she was in. Believing her to be dead, he started to turn away when he heard a low moan! Looking at her face he saw her lips move slightly and could see she was barely breathing. Letting himself down through the broken window, he found where her foot was caught and was able to free it. Then, telling the boy to pull, he, with one good arm, pushed from below until she was almost out of the car. Gil crawled out through the next window and helped the boy get his mother on out and down to the ground. Telling he boy to get back in the car and get some blankets, he tried to determine the extent of her injuries, but she was unconscious and he was not a doctor. He covered her with a blanket the boy brought and telling the boy to cover himself he said he would go for help.

Up at the top Hal had finally gotten the people quieted down and had organized the men into groups of twos. He then told the groups to stay together at all times and to make their way down to the wreckage and look for survivors. Working feverishly, they proceeded to get everyone they could find alive out, and as far away from the wreckage as possible. Using blankets they recovered from the sleeping cars, they covered them as best they could and tried to keep them calm. They had taken care of all they could see and were about to get volunteers to enter the wreckage to see if there were survivors pinned in the cars, when they heard horses coming and looked up to the top to see Wes Stone and the ranch hands pulling up in their wagons. Making his way to the top, Hal said to Wes "I don't know who you folks are, but you're a sight for sore eyes." Wes explained that he had heard the avalanche and had tried to stop the train, but the storm wouldn't co-operate. "How can we help," he asked. "We need to go through the cars" said Hal. "We've helped all who were able to get themselves out. If you have a doctor among you or even some medical supplies, there are some badly hurt people down there." "We ain't got no sawbones, but Pete here usually fixes up our broken bones and such at the ranch and he'll be glad to do what he can. We did bring all the bandages and medicine we had and we sent a rider into town for the Doctor and more help. Also, the Telegrapher has sent word to the railroad. We should get a lot of help in the next couple of hours"

As they made their way past the car which was still on the tracks to start down the slope, they heard a grating sound and saw the car lurch forward a few feet before it again stopped! Hal crawled down and went back up under the car. Crawling back out he told them some bad news. The ground under the tracks the car was on had caved in some more and if it continued, before long this car would land on the wreckage below. They had to work fast to try to save anyone trapped who was still alive, Directing some of the men to get some of the big rocks near by and shore up the tracks as best they could, Hal and Wes and the others went down the slope to the wreckage. Crawling through the twisted cars as carefully as possible, they brought out all those still alive, not bothering with the dead just now. Getting to the very bottom, Hal found Gil, the engineer with the boy and his mother. As the others carried them farther away from the train to be safe, Hal turned to leave when he heard a low moan, from near the engine. Sliding over the snow covered rocks, he found young Jimmy. He was not dead as the engineer had thought, but was still alive and pinned beneath a heavy piece of steel. With no one else close by to help, he got hold of the steel and prayed "Now Lord it's up to you". Straining with all his might he moved the heavy steel just a little and the eyes of Jimmy opened. "Can you crawl out if I get this off you"? asked Hal. "I think so" answered Jimmy. Just then came a shout from above. "Get out, get out, we can't hold this car any longer!" Ignoring the call Hal prayed once more "Help me Lord" and strained at the load. Slowly, but surely, Jimmy began to get out from beneath the weight. Just then Wes showed up and grabbing Jimmy and carrying him in his strong arms he looked at Hal and said "Come on Partner, we gotta git outta here!" As Hal tried to lay the piece of steeldown, his foot slipped and his arm was pinned under the weight. "I'm stuck" he yelled to Wes, "I'll need help to get out of here. Get that boy out quick and come back for me. When Wes was about a hundred feet away, there came another shout from above "Look out, here she comes!" Laying Jimmy safely out of the way he turned to go back but the car came crashing down and landed on top the wreckage where Hal lay with a mighty crash.

The distant sound of a train whistle told everyone that more help would be there any minute but it would be too late to help the young man who had given his life for a fellow man, The train pulled up on the east side of the wreck having come from Glenwood Springs, There was a fully outfitted hospital car, with Doctors and nurses, and soon all the survivors were safely aboard. From the west side appeared a flat car with a crane and they began the task of clearing the wreckage and removing the bodies of those who died, The body of Hal Marlin was the last one recovered. As they passed with his body, Wes Stone removed his battered cowboy hat and said "There was a MAN! He wasn't hurt in the wreck, but he organized everybody who could move into a rescue team. Without his leadership, there'd be a heap more bodies down there."

Chapter Four

At the little farm just outside Gatlinburg, Betty Marlin
was talking to Peggy Jo, the little ten year old girl from
the orphanage. Hal had made arrangements for her to
stay with Betty while he was away at the convention. They
had talked about adopting her before Betty had become
pregnant. She was a sweet child and a very good helper
to Betty around the house. "Peggy," said Betty, "we are
going to have the very best supper a man ever had ready
tomorrow night when Hal gets home." Patting her large
tummy she added "and I think little Roger is gonna need
a bright big sister like you. Would you like to be our little
girl and a big sister too?" "Oh yes" answered Peggy Jo, I'd
love it." Just then they were startled by the sound of one
of the new-fangled automobiles out in the front yard.
Looking out Betty saw that it was the Sheriff. He had one
of the few cars in the county. In Tennessee, in 1926, there
weren't many in the whole state.

Sheriff Carson walked slowly up to the door. This was
not a job he relished, and he was glad Betty wouldn't be
alone after he told her the bad news about Hal. An hour
later, he drove slowly out of the yard with tears still on his
face. He had left the telegram and the newspaper clipping
about the accident. There was nothing more he could do
for now. When he got back to town he would get some
of the ladies to come out and do whatever they could for
Betty. In her condition, she didn't need to be alone. That
baby could come just anytime.

Inside the little farm house, the world that Betty Marlin
lived in had just crumbled. It just couldn't be true, and yet

she knew it was. It was just like Hal. Reading the newspaper clipping, she was at once both proud and sad. She felt there was no way she could go on, but she knew she had to. She had a living human inside her and there was Peggy Jo. Yes she would adopt her for sure now. She'd need her.

The next morning the ladies from town came out and brought with them the letter from Hal. The one he hadn't forgot to mail this time. Later that day when she was alone for a little while, she read and re-read that letter with tears streaming down her cheeks and onto the paper. Finally, folding it neatly and putting it into the envelope along with the newspaper clipping, she put it into the big old chest and then got on her knees and said "Thank you Lord." She then called Peggy Jo and said "Come on girl, we've got work to do. If I'm not mistaken this baby will be here this time tomorrow. Ask Mrs. Johnson if she can stay the night cause her mid-wife skills will surely be needed."

Chapter Five

In the spring of 1947, Roger Marlin smiled as he walked up the lane to the little farm house where he had been born and had grown to manhood. He knew he looked trim and handsome in his navy blues but he couldn't wait to get into "Civvies" again. Standing at the door, with her hand shading her eyes of course, would be Mom. The one person in his life he always knew he could depend on. He had been too young to get in on the fighting in what they were calling World War II, but they had drafted him soon after he turned eighteen. Now at last his mandatory two years were done and he could get on with his life. His Mom came out the door and ran to meet him, huggin and kissin and talkin ninety miles an hour! After they had caught up on all the news, his Mom asked him what his plans were. "You're not gonna believe me", he said. "Try me" said Mom, "Well" he said, "do you remember how I loved going to church with you when I was little, but I rebelled when I got older? I knew I should go to church with you and I really wanted to, deep, down inside, but I just had something in me that had to rebel. Well, it's not there anymore. I'm going to seminary and I'm going into the ministry. Peggy and her husband Ward have known about this for awhile now, but I wanted to wait and surprise you when I got home." Looking for the surprise on his mother's face and in her eyes, he saw none. Instead, she was just smiling that sweet smile of hers and saying something like "I'm not a bit surprised. I gave you to God when you were born and I've always known you'd be a preacher." "Mothers", he said "are exasperating. They know everything!"

In 1953, Pastor Roger Marlin was sent to pastor a small church just west of Glenwood Springs, Colo. Yes, he knew his father had died in an accident on the railroad near there and he had accepted the position for that very reason. He would, when he had time, try to locate the scene of the accident and see if there was anyone still living near who remembered it. His mother had never talked much about his father, but she had never remarried, so he knew theirs had been a once in a lifetime thing. He remembered her saying, when he was rebelling at going to church with her as a teenager, that his father wouldn't go to church with her either, but she'd always said he was a good man and she knew he was in heaven. Now, being a Pastor, he knew that just being a good man wasn't good enough to get you into Heaven. He knew that everyone had to make Jesus Lord in their lives, repent of their sins, and, being forgiven, to do everything in their power to obey the will of the Father, if they were to be in God's kingdom. His mother said his father would not go to church with her before he died, but that she knew he was in heaven. He knew that his mother knew God's plan of salvation, so how could she believe his father was in heaven? Maybe he would find some answers near the place where his father had died.

A few weeks after he had begun pastoring the church, he was at the door afterthe service saying goodbye to the members and shaking hands, when an old cowboy shook his hand and said "Pastor, do I know you?' "Well, I've been here a few weeks now, although I don't remember seeing you before," said Roger. "Ain't been here since you been preachin," said the old cowboy, "cause I don't come real regular. I'm up at the line shack a lot of the time.

Been cowboying for better'n thirty years. Shore seems I oughta know you though. What'd you say yore name was?" "Marlin, Pastor Roger Marlin" answered Roger. He saw an amazing change come over the face of the old cowboy. "Can we talk?" asked the old man. "Just let me finish saying my goodbyes and we can. Maybe you'll stay for dinner with the wife and me."

"Reckon maybe I will" said the old cowboy, "My name's Wes Stone and I figure we got us lots to talk about." In a few minutes when Roger joined him, the cowboy said "Pastor, what's yore daddy's name?" "Well my father died near here a long time ago, but his name was Harold 'Hal' Marlin," said Roger. "Did you know him?" "I should smile I did" answered the old cowboy, "boy, er Pastor, yore daddy was the finest most decent man I ever knew and I only knowed him lessen two hours. Yuh see, I was at the train wreck that night and me'n yore daddy 'long with some others, did us some work that night. Why I reckon they called us all heroes but yore daddy was the tallest of all. I shore ain't surprised to find his boy preachin. If'n it weren't for him, don't reckon I'd a ever set foot in church myself" "There it is again," thought Roger, "this man's talking like my father was a saint, yet Mom said he wouldn't go to church with her. Wes followed him into the parsonage where he met Julie, Roger's wife, whom he had met and married while in seminary. After a good, home cooked meal, Roger and Wes set out on the porch and Wes told him all about that winter night so long ago. "Wes, you said my father was the reason you started coming to church. What did you mean?" asked Roger. "Well son, er Pastor, when we wuz getting them people out that night yore daddy would comfort them and pray over them and lead 'em to the

Lord if needed. When I seen what good he was doin and what a good man he was, I just couldn't help but want to be like him, so I asked him and he led me to the Lord. Reckon I always knowed there was someone or something bigger'n me but I didn't know Jesus and now I do. Yore daddy not only saved a lotta lives that night, but I reckon there's a heap of souls in heaven now or will be cause of yore Pa." "But mom said he wouldn't go to church with her," Roger said. "I wouldn't know nuthin boutthat," said Wes, "But yore daddy was shore a Christian and the finest man I ever knew."

Chapter Six

So here sits Roger Marlin, in the attic of the old farm, at the big old trunk that belonged to his mother reading a letter that he had never known existed. Once more he reads the handwritten lines penned so long ago:

Reno, Nev.
Nov, 18, 1926

My Darling Betty,

I have the biggest surprise for you! You have always wanted me to be an upright citizen, someone our son will be able to look up to and I have agreed with you on that score, but you have also wanted me to go to church with you and I just never could get into that religion stuff. Well, honey, the worm has turned! This past week, here in Reno, they have been having what they call a big old tent revival, just outside of town. There was a man preaching there, an evangelist they called him, and I went to hear him. Now I didn't mean to, but it was sort of a dare by one of the other salesmen. He said this man had been preaching a long time and had been to a place called the Azusa St. revival a long time ago. He said if I heard this man I would be changed forever more. So I kind a went just to show him I wasn't as gullible as some folks. Now the singing was good and the people were all jumping around sorta like at a baseball game or something. I never did know why and I was about to leave when they had what they call an 'Altar call'. Honey, people were going to that altar, that preacher was touching them, and they were falling like they'd been stoned! My buddy asked how'd I like to experience something like that, and I said it was all a show. So he said well why don't you go down there and you can show everybody it's just a show. Darling, it was the biggest mistake and the greatest thing I ever did in my life. I got saved, filled with the holy spirit and I've been every night this week. Now don't you tell me I'm crazy. I already tried telling myself. But I have actually seen people healed of all kinds of diseases, saw the blind made to see and the deaf to hear. I know it sounds crazy, but the more I get into the word of God, the more I know that that's how it's supposed to be. Honey the Lord has told me there is something big I'm supposed to do for Him real soon. I'm writing to tell you this cause I just can't hold it til I get home. We'll all be goin our separate ways tomorrow and, the Lord willing, I will see you next week. I hope that boy growing inside of you will someday feel what I feel right now. What a mighty God we serve! You know I still think we should adopt that little Peggy too. Make a good big sister. Darling, if you'll agree with me, we will dedicate our children to the lord and someday our son will be a great preacher just like the one that led me to the lord. I love you.

Your husband Hal

THE END

Christian Poetry

A *Simple Plea*

A thing so strange has come to me
and though it's real no one can see
I've lost my place, I don't belong
you see someone just took my song

I can no longer sing it seems
I can no longer dream my dreams
The spark inside no longer lives
Can't stand the pain that each day gives

So won't the one who stole my song
have pity now and right the wrong?
Please let my music live again
Let words come forth from all the pain

Let words to help someone like me
be born in all this misery
or else in sin the pain I gave
will lead me to an early grave

But wait! My cup's not empty yet
My Lord says "Son don't you forget.
I'm always there to set you free
I am the answer to your plea."

Be A Winner!

Oh Lord I cried and then I died and Satan came to call.
Said "Come on son, this time you're done and never
mind the fall."

But I said "No, I will not go. Your hell is not for me.
I'll need a spot that's not so hot for all eternity."

I said "I tried" and then I lied "I always did my best"
But I did wilt cause feeling guilt, I knew I'd failed the test.

He smiled with glee and I could see he knew that he had won
He said "It's true, I get my due cause I'm the devil son."

He takes a hold and though I'm cold I still began to sweat.
With all my might, I've got to fight. It can't be over yet.

Then as I shake, I come awake and know it's just a dream.
But still I feel it seemed so real it made me want to scream

So friend you see, it seems to me God's gave me one more shot
As if He said "Until you're dead just give it all you got.

Just give your hand to every man, show love and be a friend
If you'll be true, I'll welcome you. With me you always win!"

One Moment

So briefly held within my hand, so quickly then to leave
ere I could think to take a stand. it's promise to receive.
From whence it came and where it's gone, I cannot truly say
but only that it came alone and passed me on its way.

Though others came before this one, and more are on
the way
its passage cannot be undone, unique in its own way.
Not one is like the one before, each has its destiny.
Like grains of sand upon the shore, or rivers to the sea.

And as my mind to spirit yields, still trying to perceive,
is there a way to prove it real, or must I just believe?
And then accept the truth it brings where it be joy or strife.
it's such a sweet and precious thing, this moment we
call life.

Principles of Giving

I CAN'T REALLY GIVE 'TIL I'VE BEEN A RECEIVER
I CAN'T KNOW TRUE FAITH 'TIL I'VE BEEN A
BELIEVER
I CANNOT GIVE SOMETHING THAT I DO NOT
POSSESS
I CANNOT BLESS OTHERS IF I HAVEN'T BEEN
BLESSED

TO BE BLESSED BY THE LORD, THAT'S THE
ANSWER YOU SEE
AND TO FREELY GIVE OUT WHAT'S BEEN GIVEN
TO ME
'TIS MORE BLESSED TO GIVE THAN IT IS TO
RECEIVE
WORDS SPOKEN BY JESUS THAT I CHOOSE TO
BELIEVE

FOR RECEIVING FROM HIM IS A BLESSING YOU SEE
BUT I'M EVEN MORE BLESSED WHEN IT FLOWS
OUT THRU ME
FOR HIS WORD SAYS THAT GOD WILL OWE DEBT
TO NO MAN
AND TO GIVE IN HIS NAME IS ALL PART OF HIS PLAN

YES OUR FATHER HIMSELF, AS HE GAVE US HIS SON
DID SET THE EXAMPLE, HOW IT MUST BE DONE
THE GIFT MUST BE COSTLY TO THE GIVER YOU SEE
BUT TO THE RECEIVER, EVERY GIFT MUST BE FREE

AND THE GREATEST GIFT THAT WE COULD
POSSIBLY GIVE
IS THE STORY OF CHRIST AND THE LIFE HE DID
LIVE
IF FREELY WE WITNESS AND WE LET HIS LIGHT
SHINE
WE WILL BE PARTAKERS OF HIS GLORY DEVINE

Spring

'Tis just another day in May, a day when spring has brought
the wonder and the beauty of the world that God has
wrought.
And as, in pensive thought, I think of all that God has made,
my spirit takes me back in time to where my Lord was laid,

to a tomb that now lies empty, no body lying there,
a place where tourists gather now, to stop and pray
and stare.
And therein lies the answer in that silent, empty grave,
an earnest for the promise that our Lord and Master gave.

No other gods, so called by men, have paid that same
sweet price.
None other came to bear our sins and be our sacrifice.
That in His crimson, cleansing blood, salvation came
for all.
The only stipulation, that we all must heed His call.

For He has won the victory over death and over sin,
that we may live forever if we will be born again.
'Tis a promise He has proven that He alone could bring,
by that resurrection Sunday on a day in early spring.

The Little Girl

"LITTLE GIRL", ASKED THE MAN, AND SHE
TURNED AT THE SOUND,
"NOW WHY ARE YOU CRYIN, WITH YOUR TEARS
STREAMING DOWN?"
"IT'S A BEAUTIFUL DAY, WITH THE SUN SHINING
BRIGHT.
SO WHY ARE YOU CRYING? EVERYTHING IS ALL
RIGHT."

AS HE WAITED HER ANSWER WITH A SMILE ON
HIS FACE,
HE THOUGHT 'WHAT'S SHE DOING ALL ALONE
IN THIS PLACE?'
HE COULD SEE THAT HER DRESS WAS ALL
TATTERED AND TORN,
AND HE WONDERED WITHIN, WHY HER SHOES
WERE SO WORN.

THEN SHE SAID "NO SIR, PLEASE, EVERYTHING'S
NOT ALL RIGHT.
I'M COLD AND I'M HUNGRY AND I MUST LOOK A
SIGHT."
"IT WILL TAKE ME AWHILE TO EXPLAIN IT YOU
KNOW,
BUT IF YOU WILL LISTEN I'VE NO PLACE TO GO."

THE TEARS HAD STOPPED FALLING, SHE WAS
SERIOUS NOW.
AND HE KNEW IF HE COULD, HE MUST HELP HER
SOMEHOW.
HE TOOK OFF HIS SWEATER, WRAPPING HER ALL
AROUND,
AND THE SWEATER SO, BIG, NEARLY HUNG TO
THE GROUND

THEN HE SAID, "FIRST THINGS FIRST, THERE'S A
RESTURANT NEAR.
IF YOU'LL COME, WE CAN EAT, THEN YOUR
STORY I'LL HEAR."
WHILE THEY WALKED HE DID PRAY "FATHER,
THY WILL BE DONE
BUT FATHER WHAT'S HAPPENED TO THIS DEAR
PRECIOUS ONE?"

"SHE SEEMS SO NEGLECTED AND WITH NO ONE
TO CARE.
PLEASE HELP ME DEAR FATHER ALL HER
BURDENS TO SHARE.
MY LIFE HAS BEEN HAPPY YOU HAVE BLESSED
ME SO FREE,
WHILE THIS DEAR LITTLE CHILD LIVES IN DEEP
POVERTY."

"YOU KNOW I WOULD GIVE HER EVERYTHING THAT I OWN,
COULD I NOW BUT ERASE ALL THE SORROW SHE'S KNOWN.
I'D GIVE HER AFFECTION, LOVING HER AS MY OWN."
THEN ALL OF A SUDDEN HE COULD SEE SHE WAS GONE.

AND THEN AS FROM HEAVEN CAME A VOICE SPEAKING CLEAR,
"YOU ARE TRULY MY SON YOU NO LONGER SHALL FEAR.
FOR THIS DAY AS I CAME YOU TURNED ME NOT AWAY,
BUT INVITED ME IN AND WITH YOU I WILL STAY."

"SINCE COMPASSION YOU GAVE TO A LOST LITTLE GIRL,
THEN MAYBE, JUST MAYBE THERE'S STILL HOPE FOR THIS WORLD."

The Man

The old man sat there all alone, a sadness in his eyes.
The end was getting near he thought but then he realized.

Though death would one day take his life, it need not
be the end.
For God had given him a gift that filled the souls of men.

The words he wrote were beautiful, they soothed the
lonely heart.
For those that read were blessed by them. with love they
did impart

The very essence of his life, the thoughts he could not say.
that love he felt inside of him could see the light of day.

For deep within the soul of man there is a secret place.
Where only he and God can go. Where they meet face
to face.

And so he wrote his whole life through and shared with
those who would.
And knowing well the love of God, he did the best he could.

Though in his lifetime came not fame nor riches he
could see,
he realized at last his wealth would be eternity.

For when he walked on streets of gold from there he'd
clearly see
The words he'd written did not die. Through them,
God set men free.

Miracle In Progress

A *Study Of Truth*

For Christians who want to become more mature
in their Christian walk:

As we begin this study, I pray to our Father who is in
Heaven that His Holy Spirit will guide and direct us to the
truth that is in the Word of God. It is written that 'You shall
know the truth and the truth will set you free.' (John 8:32)
This will not be a study to search for a new interpretation
or meaning of the Word of God. No, this study is to search
the Scriptures in such a way (with the help of the Holy
Spirit) that we will find the even deeper meaning that,
to now, has been hidden from us because of our lack of
knowledge. It is written 'My people are destroyed for a
lack of knowledge'. (Hosea 4:6) It is also written 'Study to
show thyself approved unto God, a workman that needeth
not to be ashamed, rightly dividing the word of Truth'.
(2Tim. 2:15) I would also suggest, to those of you who
seek the knowledge that God has for us, that you read the
17th chapter of the Gospel of John. In that chapter, Jesus
prayed that we be one with Him and one with God the
Father. The preceding sentence is as good an example of
what I mean by understanding the deeper meaning of the
scriptures as I can think of. There is, indeed, much more
meaning to what Jesus prayed than just the surface words.
In this study, I hope that, with the help of the Holy Spirit,

we can all learn how to study in such a way that we can grasp the deeper meaning. So, can we agree that:

We are born again Christians having believed, confessed, repented, been baptized in the name of the Father, son and Holy Ghost as Jesus said and we want the fullness of all the Father has for us?

Now we are ready to proceed with our mission, which is to know, share, and live the abundant life Jesus promised us.

Before we can go deeper into all the scriptures, we must first learn what is being said in Romans 12 beginning with verse 1. Let's read it: "I beseech you therefore brethren, by the mercies of God that you present your bodies a living sacrifice, holy, acceptable unto God, which is your reasonable service. And be not conformed to this world: but be ye transformed by the renewing of your mind, that ye may prove what is that good, and acceptable, and perfect will of God" Now that is verses 1 and 2 and it is a pretty good mouthful, but can be memorized easily. If we cannot understand what these scriptures are telling us it will be much like Jesus said in Mark 4:13 "Know ye not this parable? And how then will ye know all parables." Jesus was talking about the parable of the sower and later we will talk more on this parable, but for now, we must ask the Holy Spirit to help us understand Romans 12: 1 and 2.

Before we ever even want to know more about God and His promises, one more scripture has to be opened up to us in a way that we will finally realize what God wants from us. In Phillipians 4 and verse 11, we read that Paul the apostle had to LEARN to be content in all things. God uses that scripture to let us know we have to LEARN also. And the only way to learn is by studying the word of God, not just reading it. Wow! We will see that we will have to pay close attention to every word in a scripture, not to just the main gist of the scripture. Paul was teaching on being content, but the whole sentence must be studied word by word.

Using this revelation of how to study, let's get back to Romans.

"I beseech you therefore brethren," One word at a time I (that's Paul) beseech (urge, plead, encourage) you (that's us) therefore, whoa! red flag, red flag! Any time we see a 'but' or a 'therefore' or 'finally' or any of these connecting words (called conjunctions) we must realize that in order to understand any of the following words, we must know what he just said before, so Romans 11:36 says "For of Him, and through Him, and to Him, are all things: to whom be glory for ever. Amen. Ok, that puts Romans 12 verses 1 and 2 in their proper perspective. Next word 'brethren' He is talking to believers not to the secular world. "by the mercies of God" I know that's more than one word, but for our purposes sometimes we take a phrase, It appears that what we are being 'beseeched' to do must be done through the mercies of God. Ok now the meat of the scripture, "that ye (that's us) present (give) your bodies (that us) a living sacrifice, holy, acceptable unto God, which is your reasonable service." Let's let this sentence line up with the word of God. We know, through the old testament and by the sacrifice of Jesus, God has never been willing to accept a sacrifice unless it was without blemish. That applied to the animals and it certainly applies to us. Paul is saying that only by the mercies of God. which means Jesus and His sacrifice can we even offer our bodies to God, and be accepted. If we have not been born again and cleansed by the blood of

Jesus, God cannot and will not accept any attempt by us to sacrifice an unclean vessel. And it is our reasonable service because of verse 36 in Chapter 11. Reasonable means that under the circumstances, it's the only thing that makes sense. And it is the right thing to do.

Ok, Paul is not through yet. "And be ye (that's us) not conformed to this world" (that means don't try to mix your new life with God in with the worldly way of doing things.) "But be ye transformed (be changed) by the renewing of your mind". That means forget every bit of the stinking thinking that you've been taught in this world and let God teach you a new and better way of thinking. And why this new thinking? "That ye may prove what is that good, acceptable and perfect will if God" Paul is saying that when our minds are renewed, we will prove (to ourselves) the perfect will of God. And when we present our body, a living sacrifice, holy and acceptable unto God, what we are saying is "Father, I pray that your perfect will be done in my life. I want to be in your perfect will and the only way I can know (prove) your perfect will is to be transformed by the renewing of my mind. Do you see how it all ties together? We must study so we can be aware of all that the word of God wants us to learn. It is written that the word of God is our sword of truth when we put on the whole armor of God.

And now let us return to the parable of the sower. Jesus said we must plant the seed (the word of God) in good ground. The good ground is our hearts (not the ones beating but the center of our being. our spirits.) It is written God is Spirit and we must worship Him in Spirit and in truth. We were made in the image of God and since God is Spirit, it is our spirit that was made in His image. Ok if we must worship Him in spirit and in truth, how do we do that? Our spirit is our innermost being and the truth is the word of God. So according to the parable of the sower, we must plant the word of God in our spirit which is our good ground. It is written 'As a man thinketh in his heart, so is he" Why do we need the word of God growing in our heart, spirit, innermost being? In Prove. 4 beginning in verse 20 we read: "My son, attend to my words; incline thine ear unto my sayings. Let them not depart from thine eyes; keep them in the midst of thine heart. For they are life unto those who find them, and health to all their flesh." WOW! Who in their right mind would not want life and health? So, again Brethren, I beseech you to learn the word of God so that it may be planted in the good ground of you innermost being, your spirit.

May God bless you all.

Missed Opportunities

Today, December 20th, 2003. One week ago today, I had my 76th birthday and I felt old. This morning, I have spent the hours listening to the best music this side of heaven and I don't feel old at all. As I listened to the wonderful songs. I gazed around the apartment, looking at the computer, the television, the kitchen and all the things that make a place, or home, come alive. And I realized that very soon or, someday soon, the apartment would change. I would, for one reason or another, be gone and the apartment, at least for awhile, would be empty and not alive at all. The same windows, the same doors, the same floors and ceilings would be here, but without an occupant, the apartment would not be alive. And it came to me, that the same is true of our bodies. Without an occupant, they are not alive. Now, of course, occupant is just another word for spirit. The songs I listened to were gospel songs on Gaither videos. And, as I said, there is no better or sweeter music than songs about, to, and for, God. Worshiping God in song always brings His presence and it is the closest we can get this side of Heaven.

As I pondered these thoughts in my mind, I realized that we all take so much for granted in this life. An empty building, home or apartment can, of course, be filled with another occupant and so, we do not mourn empty spaces just because they are empty. Unless they are empty because we have just lost a loved one and then that makes all the difference. We do, however, always mourn the empty body (death) because it cannot be filled with another spirit. As I remembered back to my childhood, all the loved ones of my past came drifting through my memory, bringing tears, smiles, joy and sadness. I thought of my father, my mother and others of my family, and of what I would say to them now, if only they were still alive. I do not mean to say that there were too many things I left unsaid when they were here. It's just that I long for that privilege I once had. It seems when we are young, we are so full of our own lives, our dreams, our aspirations, that we tend to neglect the older ones in our families. As we grow older (and hopefully, wiser) we remember the opportunities we had to question or just fellowship with our parents or grandparents or aunts and uncles, and realize that there was so much more we could have learned from them. And, I, for one, would love to be able to have my loved ones see what God has done in my life.

As I approach (or live in) the twilight of my years, I realize, more than ever before, the enormity of life. In our humanity, it is very easy to lose focus on God and focus on the material and human things in this life. As we grow old and realize that death awaits us all, it is a bit easier to think about our creation and about God and who He is. The saddest thing about this, is that we are never promised that we will grow old enough to change our focus, and even if we do, I think of the wasted life we leave behind us because we would not let God be even a part of our lives. Yes, there are a lot of questions I would love to be able to ask of loved ones who have gone on. About life in general, about their lives, their thoughts and a myriad of other things, but mostly, I just wish I could sit down and talk to my dad about God. Yes, they got old, or so it seemed at the time, but now that I am there I know they didn't stop living just because they were old. Did they get grouchy, forgetful, sloppy and sometimes, embarrassing? Yes, but that's no reason to write them off. Will what I'm writing change the way young people treat older people? Probably not, but if just one youngster is encouraged to sit and visit with an older relative, then this will have had a purpose for being written. God bless everyone.

The Love Of God

This is a day like any other day and yet, is it? I am a man like any other man and yet, am I? Is there any sameness in God's mercies? His word says His mercies are new every day. Therefore the scripture "This is a day the Lord hath made, I will rejoice and be glad in it." takes on a different meaning. I have felt a burning deep within me to write something about God's truth for a long time now, and yet I have had to wait for God to deal with me to the extent He has finally been able to get me to understand what we are all about. The Apostle Paul continually exhorted in his letters that nothing be preached except the gospel of Christ and Him crucified. Jesus himself said Go ye into all the world and TEACH and PREACH the good news (Gospel) to all nations. God has revealed to me that we men, with our traditions, have really strayed far from His commandments. First, the church. We, my brothers and sisters, are the church. The Holy Word of God says that we (our bodies) are the temple of God, yet the traditions of men have made the church into an edifice, a building, a designated place of worship. Think of that! Jesus said where two or more are gathered in my name, there I will be also. Yes, the word of God says to forsake not the assembling together of yourselves but I cannot read where we are to assemble in a building, built with millions of dollars that could have been used to feed widows and orphans or to help our fellow Christians, and I do not believe you can read that either. Somewhere, over the centuries since the crucifixion of Christ, we have somehow decided that more is better. We (men) have decided that we need to build huge buildings that will hold more people so we can minister to more people at one time, and collect more money to do more things, things which almost never get done. Large salaries for Pastors, (Senior, Associate, Youth and Children's) contributions for Evangelists, Quartets, Singers and various other 'Ministries' and of course the cost of the building, maintenance, fellowship diners, etc. seem to leave little to do benevolent work.

I know I am taking on some 'Sacred cows' and by now some of you will be saying things like; 'This guy is really anti-church' or 'who does he think he is. Such teaching, if believed, would create an economical disaster. We can't destroy the lives of people who have devoted their lives to doing the work of God.' Wait. What is the work of God? What is our purpose on this earth?

Let's take some of the things we have already mentioned, one at a time.

First, 'More is better". Stop and think. If EVERY born again Christian would make a commitment to lead at least one other sinner to the Lord, see him or her saved and living in the body of Christ, what would happen? The church (body of Christ) would just keep doubling in a domino effect until there would be no more sinners! I submit to you that God did not and does not intend for His church (the body of Christ) to be filled with members who go to "church" on Sundays, Wednesdays and special times, sit on the pew and dutifully listen to the preacher, pay their tithes, fellowship with other brothers and sisters at lunch and then NEVER have the most wonderful experience in the world, that is, leading another to Christ. I believe that the bible is obviously teaching us in the New Testament, that believers met in homes for the edifying of each other, to exhort one another, to prepare each other for the work there is to be done. This was assembling together of yourselves. The work to be done is the witnessing to others the 'good news' the gospel of Christ. We, my friends, don't save anybody. God does that. We are only the messengers or vessels He uses. Therefore, a one on one 'ministry' where questions can be asked and answered is much more effective than one man preaching to ten thousand. In answering possible questions or objections to what I am writing, I am not trying to be argumentative, or confrontational. I am merely writing as the Holy Spirit directs. So, some may ask, "OK, what about Peter preaching to three thousand on the day of Pentecost?" I submit to you the word says Peter preached to a crowd, not three thousand. What do you think the other Apostles were doing? I believe the three thousand souls that were added that day were ministered to in small groups by the other apostles and believers. "OK, what about Eph. 4;11?" I suggest you follow 4;ll by also reading 4;12 and then I believe you will see that smaller groups would be the only effective way for the "five fold ministry" to work. But enough of this! If you really want to know what God wants, ask Him. His word says 'If any lack wisdom, let him ask of the Father who gives to all men liberally'.

Finally, let me close this epistle with this. It's all about LOVE. For God so LOVED the world, . . . If you love me you will keep my commandments, . . . If I have faith to remove mountains and have not LOVE I am nothing, Now abides faith, hope, and LOVE and the greatest of these is

LOVE, . . . behold what manner of LOVE this is that we should be called the sons of God. Yes, God's word is full of promises. Yes He would that we prosper as our souls prosper. Yes, the same works Jesus did, they that follow Him shall do and even greater works in His name. Yes, we can lay hands on the sick and pray for them and they shall be healed. Yes, ALL of God's promises are true.

But as Paul wrote in first Corinthians, 13;1, Though I speak with the tongues of men and of angels and have not LOVE, I am become as sounding brass, or a tinkling cymbal. And though I have the gift of prophecy, and understand all mysteries, and all knowledge, and though I have all faith, so that I could remove mountains, and have not LOVE, I am nothing. We cannot please God without faith and I am convinced we cannot please Him without LOVE.

We, as men, with our traditions and conditions, have made it almost impossible for sinners to hear and understand the good news or gospel. I beseech you therefore brethren, search your own hearts and ask the Father to reveal through the Holy Spirit, what your needs are in order to be the person He wants you to be, and then ask Him to supply those needs and He will not fail you. May God richly bless those who take the time to read this epistle.

You Shall Know The Truth And The Truth Shall Set You Free

Hello friends. Have you ever wished your life could be free from stress? Good, you've come to the right place! Have you ever wanted to be free from worry and fear? Again, you've come to the right place. Have you ever longed for a peace so wonderful that there was no way to explain it? A peace that could be experienced but could not be understood? You've got it. You are at the right place. OK, we're going to take a little journey, but before you decide 'this guy is nuts' or 'I wonder what's in it for him' or 'he must believe in magic', let me make one thing perfectly clear. First, there is no money or cost involved in this (except your time) and I don't believe in magic, but I must admit that, according to the world's idea of logic, I am nuts! Still with me? Good. By the title, I believe most of you will have guessed that this is about God and His love letter to us, the Bible. I make no apologies for that. I pray the you will continue.

As a start, I am going to list a few of the promises in the Holy word of God. (Well, several actually) I could give book chapter and verse, but I believe the Holy Spirit, who is leading me in this endeavor, has said "No!" :

> "For God so loved the world that He gave His only begotten son, that whosoever believed in Him should not perish, but have everlasting life."

"and lo, I am with you always, even to the end of the world."

"Never will I leave you; never will I forsake you."

"Fear not: for I have redeemed thee, I have called thee by thy name; thou are mine."

"neither give place to the devil."

"Submit yourselves therefore to God. Resist the devil and he will flee."

"Be anxious for nothing"

"In this world you will have tribulations, but fear not for I have overcome the world."

"And the peace of God, which passes all understanding, shall keep your hearts and mind, through Christ Jesus."

"By His stripes, ye were healed"

"By this shall they know that ye are my disciples, that ye have love for one another."

"I can do all things through Christ who strengthens me."

"No weapon formed against thee shall prosper."

OK, I'm not going to rewrite the Holy Bible. I will, however, try to explain a few things to you which I believe the Holy Spirit has revealed to me. Now, don't get huffy! He will also reveal the same things to you. You only have to ask. First, let me say God does not want us to walk in fear. When you have the time, run references in the Bible concerning fear and I believed you will be amazed. Also, God does not want us to have stress or worry in our lives. Yes, bad things happen to good people. Yes, we are in this world, but we do not have to be of this world. Paul said "I have LEARNED to be content in all things." So it is a learning process. How do we learn? By reading God's word and praying, then obeying and trusting. God has said He will supply our every need. If any lack wisdom, we are told to ask God for it. Now, I am going to share with you a prayer that I believe will completely change your life (as God sees the need for change) and I also believe this prayer must come from your heart with no 'buts' or conditions. We must make Jesus, Lord of our lives, submit and surrender completely to His will and He will not fail us!

So please pray with me:

Our Father which art in Heaven, hallowed be thy name. Thy Kingdom come, thy will be done on earth as it is in Heaven. Father, I completely submit my will to yours and surrender every thing in my life to you. I ask, Holy Father, that you cleanse me of all imperfections, sins and any 'idols' I have placed before you. Father, I want to be the person you created me to be. I want to do the things you've prepared for me to do and I want to say the things you want me to say. Father, when I begin to lose focus on you, let your Holy Spirit guide me back to the right path. When I pray for anything, let me always end my prayer with 'nevertheless, not my will, but thine be done.' Let me obey your instructions to me through the Holy Spirit and let me trust You to know far better than I what my needs are and that You will supply them. Let the words of your promises be written on my heart and, Lord, lead me gently to that place of intimacy with you that gives me the peace that passes understanding and freedom from worry, stress and fear. And Father, as I close my prayer, let me not forget to thank you for everything you've already done in my life and let me never forget to give all the glory and honor to you. Amen!

Now, you will not find my name or anything about me anywhere in this letter. You see, it's not about me, it's about God. Jesus died for your sins, I couldn't if I wanted to. I also ask that, if you feel the urging of the Holy Spirit, please pass this on, freely and with my own urging, to someone else and ask them to do the same as they are lead by the Spirit. God Bless each and everyone who reads this! Amen

Where Is The Contentment?

WHEN WE ASK "WHERE IS THE CONTENTMENT" WE ARE ACTUALLY ASKING "WHERE IS THE LOVE". YOU CANNOT HAVE ONE WITHOUT THE OTHER. THIS WILL BE THE BASIC CONTEXT OF THIS MESSAGE. AS I PASS THROUGH THESE, THE LATTER YEARS OF MY JOURNEY ON THIS EARTH, I WILL ENDEAVOR TO SHARE WITH YOU ALL OF THE CLEAR MESSAGE THE FATHER HAS GIVEN ME IN HELPING ME PREPARE FOR THE CROSSING OF JORDAN. WITH ALL PRAISE AND GLORY TO GOD THE FATHER, I CAN TRUTHFULLY SAY I DO NOT FEAR THE END OF THIS LIFE, BUT RATHER LOOK FORWARD TO THE BEGINNING OF THE NEXT.

IT IS WITH HUMILITY THAT I UNDERTAKE THIS TASK WHICH, I BELIEVE, HAS BEEN GIVEN TO ME BY GOD. I FERVENTLY PRAY THAT THE HOLY SPIRIT WILL LEAD (GUIDE AND DIRECT) ME IN ALL THINGS I SAY, FOR "AS MANY AS ARE LED BY THE SPIRIT OF GOD, THEY ARE THE SONS OF GOD". Ro. 8:14

I WANT YOU TO PAY VERY CLOSE ATTENTION NOW TO WHAT I AM ABOUT TO SAY. THIS COULD VERY WELL BE THE MOST IMPORTANT THING YOU WILL LEARN SINCE YOU BEGAN YOUR WALK WITH GOD. THE WORD OF GOD SAYS "BLESSED ARE THEY WHICH DO HUNGER AND THIRST AFTER RIGHTEOUSNESS, FOR THEY SHALL BE

FILLED" Matt. 5:6 IN TODAY'S WORLD, I HEAR SO MANY 'CHRISTIANS' WHO ALMOST ALWAYS COMPLETELY MIS-QUOTE OR MIS-UNDERSTAND THIS SCRIPTURE. THEY SAY THEY ARE HUNGERING OR THIRSTING TO HAVE A MINISTRY, OR SEE A MOVE OF THE SPIRIT, OR WITNESS A MIRACLE OR RECEIVE THE PROSPERITY GOD HAS PROMISED TO HIS CHILDREN.

AS YOU ARE HEARING THIS YOU ARE PROBABLY THINKING 'WHAT'S WRONG WITH THAT?' I AM GLAD YOU ASKED! THIS SCRIPTURE IS NOT TALING ABOUT HUNGERING OR THIRSTING FOR THINGS! IT SAYS 'RIGHTEOUSNESS'. AND WHAT YOU MAY ASK IS RIGHTEOUSNESS? IT IS RIGHT STANDING WITH GOD. IT MEANS DOING, AND BELIEVING IN, THE PERFECT WILL OF GOD NO MATTER WHAT THE CIRCUMSTANCES OR SITUATION MAY BE. UH OH, THAT BRINGS OUT THE STATEMENT 'IT IS NOT IN GOD'S WILL FOR HIS CHILDREN TO SUFFER!' HMMM, WONDER WHAT THE EARLY APOSTLES OR PAUL OR THE FIRST CENTURYCHRISTIANS WOULD HAVE TO SAY ABOUT THAT? AND WHAT DID JESUS MEAN WHEN HE SAID "IN THIS WORLD YOU WILL HAVE TRIBULATIONS"? YOU SEE, WE DON'T SEEK GOD SO WE CAN BE FREE FROM ALL THE PROBLEMS THAT CONFRONT THE SECULAR WORLD EACH AND EVERY DAY. JESUS SAID "SEEK YE FIRST THE KINGDOM OF GOD AND HIS RIGHTEOUSNESS". THERE'S THAT WORD AGAIN! IF WE ARE TO BE THE PERSON GOD CREATED US TO BE, WE MUST ACCEPT GOD AS HE IS, WHICH INCLUDES BUT IS NOT LIMITED TO ACCEPTING JESUS AS LORD

AND HIS SACRIFICE AND BEING OBEDIENT TO HIS EVERY COMMANDMENT. YOU SEE, JESUS SAID THE GREATEST COMMANDMENT IS TO "LOVE THE LORD THY GOD WITH ALL THY HEART AND WITH ALL THY SOUL AND WITH ALL THY MIND." AND THE SECOND GREATEST COMMANDMENT IS TO "LOVE THY NEIGHBOR AS THYSELF". IF WE ARE OBEDIENT IN THESE TWO COMMANDMENTS, WE CANNOT FAIL! FOR JESUS SAID "ON THESE TWO COMMANDMENTS HANG ALL THE LAW AND THE PROPHETS."

THESE SCRIPTURES ARE FOUND IN THE 22ND CHAPTER OF MATTHEW. LET'S TAKE A LOOK AT THESE SCRIPTURES AND BREAK THEM DOWN SO WE CAN UNDERSTAND WHAT HE IS SAYING. 'WITH ALL OUR MIND', WHAT DOES THAT MEAN? IT MEANS GETTING TO KNOW GOD AND HIS LAWS AND WAYS OF DOING THINGS BY STUDYING HIS WORD AND BY RENEWING OUR MINDS. 'WITH ALL OUR HEART AND ALL OUR SOUL, WHAT DOES THAN MEAN? THAT MEANS WHEN OUR MINDS HAVE BEEN RENEWED, WE WILL HAVE A DIVINE NATURE (2ND Ptr. 1:4) AND WE WILL SEE THINGS AS GOD SEES THEM AND REACT TO THEM THE WAY GOD WOULD. WE CANNOT STOP AT JUST BELIEVING GOD IS. WE MUST GET TO KNOW HIM SO WELL THAT IT WILL BE OUT NATURE TO BELIEVE ALL THAT HE IS, SAYS AND DOES. IT WILL BECOME A WAY OF LIFE.

YOU SEE, ONLY WHEN WE GET TO THE POINT THAT GOD'S RIGHTEOUSNESS IS SUFFICIENT FOR US WILL WE STOP PUTTING SO MUCH EMPHASIS ON THINGS. JESUS SAID 'ALL THESE THINGS WILL

BE ADDED UNTO YOU.' AND GOD'S WORD SAYS 'MY GOD SHALL SUPPLY ALL YOUR NEED ACCORDING TO HIS RICHES IN GLORY BY CHRIST JESUS' Phil. 4:19 IF YOU REALLY LOVE GOD YOU WILL BELIEVE THAT SCRIPTURE. AND IF YOU REALLY BELIEVE THAT SCRIPTURE, YOU WILL STOP ASKING FOR THINGS YOU THINK YOU NEED AND JUST SAY 'MY GOD WILL SUPPLY ALL MY NEEDS'AND THEN TRUST HIM!

MY FRIENDS, WE CANNOT HAVE IT TWO WAYS. WE EITHER TRUST GOD OR WE DON'T. JUST BECAUSE THE CIRCUMSTANCES MAY LOOK DIRE OR THE SITUATION SCARY, WE CAN'T NOT TRUST GOD. ONLY BY TRUSTING THE FATHER COMPLETELY CAN WE FIND THE CONTENTMENT PAUL TALKED ABOUT WHEN HE WROTE 'I HAVE LEARNED, IN WHATEVER STATE I AM IN, THEREWITH TO BE CONTENT. NOTICE, IT IS SOMETHING WE HAVE TO LEARN. JESUS SAID MANY TIMES IN THE WORD SOMETHING TO THE EFFECT 'THY FAITH HATH MADE THE WHOLE'. NOTICE, HE DIDN'T SAY 'I MADE YOU WHOLE' OR 'GOD MADE YOU WHOLE', BUT YOUR FAITH. THE KIND OF FAITH JESUS WAS TALKING ABOUT WAS BELIEVING GOD SAID WHAT HE MEANT AND MEANT WHAT HE SAID. SURE THE SCRIPTURE SAYS 'BY HIS STRIPES YE ARE HEALED', BUT LIKE 'WHOSOEVER BELIEVES ON HIM' IT MEANS NOTHING IF WE DON'T LEARN AND ACCEPT THE WHOLE PACKAGE GOD IS OFFERING US. EVERY BLESSING FROM GOD IS BASED ON OUR FAITH AND OBEDIENCE AND OUR SACRIFICE. PAUL WROTE 'IT IS NOT I THAT LIVETH, BUT CHRIST THAT LIVETH

IN ME'. FRIENDS WE ARE MORE CONCERNED WITH OUR BODILY COMFORTS AND WELL BEING THAN WE ARE IN OFFERING OUR BODIES AS A LIVING SACRIFICE AND THEN TRUSTING GOD TO MEET OUR NEEDS.

WE HUMANS BELIEVE THAT SICKNESSES, DISEASES, ACCIDENTS, ALL OF WHICH CAN LEAD TO DEATH, ARE TERRIBLE AND CANNOT BE IN THE WILL OF GOD. PAUL WROTE 'FOR ME TO DIE IS GAIN, BUT TO LIVE IS CHRIST'. THIS MEANS WE ARE NO LONGER HELD TO (SPIRITUAL) DEATH IN OUR SINS BUT THROUGH CHRIST WE HAVE (EVERLASTING, SPIRITUAL) LIFE. DOES THIS COME AUTOMATICALLY? NO. WE HAVE TO HEAR, BELIEVE, CONFESS AND ACCEPT JESUS AS LORD OF OUR LIVES. WE DIDN'T AND DON'T TELL GOD HOW TO SAVE US. WE ACCEPT HIS PLAN AND WILL. THE SAME IS TRUE OF EVERY OTHER PROBLEM THIS LIFE CAN THROW OUR WAY. THROUGH THE MIGHTY LOVE OF GOD THAT COURSES THROUGH OUR VERY BEINGS (WE WERE MADE IN HIS IMAGE AND LIKENESS AND HE IS SPIRIT AND HE IS LOVE) WE CAN LEARN TO RETURN THAT LOVE TO HIM AND SO RECEIVE HIS PERFECT WILL FOR OUR LIVES, WHATEVER THAT MAY BE. AND BY RETURNING THAT LOVE WE WILL FIND THE CONTENTMENT WE ARE SEEKING, BECAUSE WE KNOW THE END OF THE STORY AND WE WON'T LET CIRCUMSTANCES OR SITUATIONS WORRY US. REMEMBER, BE ANXIOUS FOR NOTHING. GOD BLESS.